The bus got very quiet.

And everybody kept on waiting and waiting for me to say the name of my job.

Except for I just couldn't think of anything.

And so my face got very reddish and hottish.

And I felt like P.U. again.

"See? Told ja!" said that mean Jim. "There is no such job! Told ja! Told ja! Told ja!"

After that I sat down very quiet. And I stared out the window.

'Cause the sickish feeling was back inside my stomach again, that's why.

Me and my big fat mouth.

The Junie B. Jones series by Barbara Park

Junie B. Jones
and her
Big Fat Mouth

by Barbara Park
illustrated by Denise Brunkus

RANDOM HOUSE AUSTRALIA

Random House Australia Pty Ltd
20 Alfred Street, Milsons Point, NSW 2061
http://www.randomhouse.com.au

Sydney   New York   Toronto
London   Auckland   Johannesburg

'Junie B. Jones and her Big Fat Mouth' first published in
the United States in 1993 by Random House, Inc.

Text copyright © 1993 by Barbara Park
Illustrations copyright © 1993 by Denise Brunkus

Random House Australia Edition 2003
Reprinted 2003

National Library of Australia
Cataloguing-in-Publication Data

       Park, Barbara.
       Junie B. Jones and her big fat mouth.

       For children aged 6+.
       ISBN 1 74051 880 2 (pbk.).

       1. Jones, Junie B. (Fictitious character) - Juvenile
       fiction. 2. Occupations - Juvenile fiction. 3.
       Kindergarten - Juvenile fiction. 4. Schools - Juvenile
       fiction. I. Brunkus, Denise. II. Title. (Series : Park,
       Barbara. Junie B. Jones ; 3).

    813.54

Printed and bound by Griffin Press Pty Ltd, Adelaide

Contents

Junie B. Jones
and her
Big Fat Mouth

1/Punishment

My name is Junie B. Jones. The B stands for Beatrice. Except I don't like Beatrice. I just like B and that's all.

I go to kindergarten. My room is named Room Nine. There are lots of rules in that place.

Like no shouting.

And no running in the hall.

And no butting the other children in the stomach with your head.

My teacher's name is Mrs.

She has another name, too. But I just like Mrs. and that's all.

Last week Mrs. clapped her loud hands together. Then she made a 'nouncement to us.

A *'nouncement* is the school word for telling us something very important.

"Boys and girls. May I have your attention, please?" she said. "Today is going to be a special day in Room Nine. We're going to be talking about different careers you can have when you grow up."

"Yeah, only guess what?" I said. "I never even heard of that dumb word careers before. And so I won't know what the heck we're talking about."

Mrs. made squinty eyes at me. "A career

is a *job*, Junie B.," she said. "And please raise your hand before you speak."

Then Mrs. talked some more about careers. And she said Monday was going to be called Job Day. And everybody in Room Nine would come to school dressed up like what kind of job they wanted to be.

After that, Room Nine was very excited. Except for not me. 'Cause I had a big problem, that's why.

"Yeah, only guess what?" I said. "I don't know what I want to be when I grow up. And so that means I can't come to school on Monday. And now I'll probably flunk kindergarten."

"Hurray!" shouted a mean boy named Jim.

I made a fist at him. "How'd you like a

knuckle sandwich, you big fat Jim?" I shouted right back.

Mrs. came over to my table. She bended down next to me.

"*Please,* Junie B. You simply must try to control yourself better in class. We've talked about this before, remember?"

"Yes," I said nicely. "Only I hate that dumb guy."

Just then my bestest friend Lucille—who sits next to me—stood up and fluffed her ruffly dress.

"I always control myself, don't I, Teacher?" she said. "That's because my nanna taught me to act like a little lady. And so Junie B. Jones should act more like me."

I made a growly face at her. "I *do* act like a little lady, you dumb bunny Lucille! And

4

don't say that again, or I'll knock you on your can."

Mrs. did a frown at me.

"Just kidding," I said very quick.

Except for Mrs. kept on frowning. And then she gave me punishment.

Punishment is the school word for sitting at a big table all by yourself.

And everybody keeps on staring at you.

And it makes you feel like P.U.

That's how come I put my head down on the table. And I covered it up with my arms.

'Cause punishment takes the friendly right out of you.

And so at recess I didn't speak to Lucille. And I didn't speak to my other bestest friend named Grace, either.

I just sat down in the grass all by myself.

And I watched Janitor paint the litter cans.

And I played with a stick and an ant and that's all.

"I hate Room Nine," I said very grumpity.

Except for just then I saw something very wonderful in the grass! And its name was two cherry Life Savers!

"Hey! I love those guys!" I said.

Then I quick picked one up. And I blowed off the germs. And I put it right in my mouth.

"WAIT! DON'T DO THAT!" shouted a loud voice at me. "SPIT THAT OUT RIGHT NOW!"

I turned my head.

It was Janitor! He was running at me speedy quick. His jingly keys were jangling all

over the place.

"SPIT THAT OUT, I SAID!" he yelled again.

And so then I spit the cherry Life Saver on the ground. 'Cause the guy was scaring me, that's why.

Janitor bended down next to me.

"I didn't mean to frighten you, sis," he said. "But I spotted a bunch of dirty candy in the grass. And I was going to clean it up when I finished painting."

He looked serious at me. "Don't you ever eat anything you find on the ground. Do you hear? Not *ever*."

"But I blowed off the germs," I told him.

Janitor shook his head. "You can't blow germs off," he said. "Eating things that you find on the ground is very, very dangerous."

Then Janitor picked up the dangerous candy. "Now run along and play," he said.

I did a big sigh. "Yeah, only I can't," I said.

"'Cause I shot off my big fat mouth in kindergarten. And then I got punishment. And now I hate my bestest friend Lucille."

Janitor smiled a little bit sad. "Life is hard sometimes, isn't it, sis?" he said.

I bobbed my head up and down. "Yes," I said. "Life is P.U."

Then Janitor patted my head and he walked away.

And so guess what?

I just like Janitor.

And that's all.

2/The Cop and Dr. Smiley

When we came in from recess, Mrs. was clapping her loud hands together again.

"Boys and girls, please take your seats quickly! I've got a wonderful surprise for you!"

Then I got very excited inside my stomach! Because surprises are my most favorite things in the whole world!

"IS IT JELLY DOUGHNUTS?" I shouted.

Mrs. put her finger to her lips. That means *be quiet*.

"YEAH, ONLY GUESS WHAT? JELLY DOUGHNUTS ARE MY MOST FAVORITE KIND OF DOUGHNUTS! EXCEPT I ALSO LIKE THE CREAMY KIND. AND THE CHOCOLATE KIND! AND THE KIND WITH RAINBOW SPRINKLES ON THE TOP!"

After that, my mouth got very watering. And some drool fell on the table.

I wiped it up with my sweater sleeve.

Just then there was a knock on the door.

Mrs. hurried to open it.

"HEY! IT'S A COP!" I hollered very excited.

The cop came into Room Nine.

He had on a blue shirt with a shiny badge. And shiny black boots. And a shiny white motorcycle helmet.

Mrs. smiled. "Boys and girls, I would like you to meet my friend, Officer Mike. Officer Mike is a policeman. Who can tell me what policemen do?"

"I can!" I called out. "They rest people! 'Cause one time some cops rested a guy on my street. And so that means they made him take a nap, I think."

Just then that Jim I hate laughed very loud.

"They didn't *rest* him, stupid!" he hollered. "They *arrested* him! That means they took him to jail. And so your neighbor's a dirty rotten jailbird!"

Then the other kids laughed too. And so I hided my head.

"Yeah, only I hardly even know the guy," I said to just myself.

After that, Officer Mike took off his shiny white helmet. And he told us some other stuff that cops do. Like give our dads speeding tickets. And rest drunk guys.

Also he let us play with his handcuffs and his shiny white helmet. Except for the helmet was very too big for my head. And it covered my whole entire eyes.

"HEY! WHO TURNED OUT THE LIGHTS?" I said.

'Cause that was a funny joke, of course.

Then another knock came at the door.

This time it was a lady in a long white jacket. She was carrying a giant red toothbrush.

"Boys and girls, this is Dr. Smiley," said Mrs. "Dr. Smiley is a children's dentist."

Dr. Smiley hung up some posters of teeth. Then she talked all about Mr. Tooth Decay. And she said to brush our teeth at night. And also in the morning.

"Yeah, 'cause if you don't brush in the morning, your breath smells like stink," I said.

After that I showed Dr. Smiley my wiggling tooth.

"Losing baby teeth is exciting, isn't it?" she asked.

"Yes," I said. "Except for I don't like the part where you cry and spit blood."

Dr. Smiley made a sick face. Then she passed out minty green dental floss. And all the kids in Room Nine practiced flossing.

Flossing is when you pull strings through your mouth.

Only pretty soon an accident happened.

That's because a boy named William winded his floss too tight. And his teeth and head got in a tangled knot ball. And Dr. Smiley couldn't undo him.

Then Mrs. had to call Janitor speedy quick. And so he runned to Room Nine. And he shined his giant flashlight in William's mouth.

And then Dr. Smiley got the dangerous floss right out of there!

Room Nine clapped and clapped.

Dr. Smiley did a bow.

Then Mrs. said that maybe some of us might like to dress up like dentists or police officers on Job Day.

"Yeah, only what if you don't like drunk guys or bloody teeth?" I asked.

Mrs. rolled her eyes way up at the ceiling. Then she walked Officer Mike and Dr. Smiley out into the hall.

That's when Room Nine started buzzing very loud.

Buzzing is what you do when your teacher leaves the room.

"I'm going to dress up like an actress on Job Day," said a girl named Emily.

"I'm going to dress up like a princess," said my bestest friend Lucille that I hate.

I did a giggle. "I'm going to dress up like a bullfighter!" I said.

Then I ran speedy fast around the room. And I butted that mean Jim in the stomach with my head.

And guess what?

I didn't even get caught!

That's what!

3 / Me and My Big Fat Mouth

After school was over, me and my bestest friend named Grace walked to the bus together.

Except for that Grace kept on wanting to skip. And I didn't.

"How come you don't want to skip?" she said. "Me and you always skip to the bus."

"I know, Grace," I said. "But today I've got a very big problem inside my head. And it's called I still don't know what job I want to be when I grow up."

"I do," said that Grace. "I'm going to be Mickey Mouse at Disneyland."

I did a big sigh at her. "Yeah, only too bad for you, Grace," I said. "'Cause there's only one real alive Mickey Mouse. And you're not him."

That Grace laughed very hard.

"Mickey isn't *real*, silly. He's just a mouse suit with a guy inside," she said.

And so just then I felt very sickish inside of my stomach.

'Cause I didn't know Mickey was a suit, that's why.

"What did you have to tell me that for, Grace?" I said real upset. "Now I feel very depressed."

Then I hurried up on the bus. And I scooted way over by the window.

Except I couldn't get any peace and quiet. 'Cause everybody kept on talking about dumb old Job Day.

"I'm going to be a famous singer," said a girl named Rose.

"I'm going to be a famous baton twirler," said another girl named Lynnie.

Then a girl named Charlotte said she was going to be a famous painter. "Famous painters are called artists," she explained. "And artists are very rich."

After that I felt a little bit cheerier. 'Cause guess what? Grandma Miller says I paint beautifully, that's what.

"Hey. Maybe I'll be a famous painter too," I said.

"I'm gonna be a prison guard," said a boy named Roger. "My uncle Roy is a prison guard. And he gets to carry the keys for the whole entire prison."

Then my mouth did a smile. 'Cause one time my dad gave me the key to the front door. And I unlocked it all by myself. And I didn't even need any help!

"Hey. Maybe I might carry keys too, Roger," I said. "'Cause I know how to use those things very good."

Just then William raised his hand very bashful. "I'm going to be a superhero and save people from danger," he said.

And so then I jumped right out of my seat! 'Cause that was the bestest idea of all!

"Me too, William!" I hollered. "'Cause that sounds very exciting, I think. And so I'm going to save people from danger too!"

Then that mean Jim jumped up at me. "Copycat! Copycat! You're just copying everybody else. And anyway, you can't be three jobs! You can only be one!"

I made a growly face at him.

"I *am* just being one job!" I said very

angry. "It's a special kind of job where you paint and you unlock stuff and you save people! So there! Ha-ha on you!"

That Jim made a cuckoo sign at me.

"Goonie," he said. "Goonie B. Jones. There's no such job like that in the whole entire universe!"

"YES, THERE IS! THERE IS TOO,

YOU BIG FAT JIM!" I yelled. "AND IT'S THE BESTEST JOB IN THE WHOLE WIDE WORLD!"

He crossed his arms and did a mean smile.

"Okay. Then what's the name of it?" he said.

Then the bus got very quiet.

And everybody kept on waiting and waiting for me to say the name of my job.

Except for I just couldn't think of anything.

And so my face got very reddish and hottish.

And I felt like P.U. again.

"See? Told ja!" said that mean Jim. "There is no such job! Told ja! Told ja! Told ja!"

After that I sat down very quiet. And I stared out the window.

'Cause the sickish feeling was back inside my stomach again, that's why.

Me and my big fat mouth.

4/Dumb Ollie

I got off the bus at my corner. Then I runned to my house speedy quick.

"HELP! HELP! I'M IN BIG TROUBLE!" I yelled to Mother. "'CAUSE I ACCIDENTALLY SHOT OFF MY BIG FAT MOUTH ON THE BUS! AND NOW I HAVE TO PAINT AND UNLOCK STUFF AND SAVE PEOPLE FROM DANGER! ONLY WHAT KIND OF STUPID DUMB JOB IS THAT?"

"Back here," called Mother.

Back here means the nursery. The nursery is the place where my new baby brother named Ollie lives.

I ran there my very fastest.

Mother was rocking Ollie in the rocking chair. He was a little bit sleeping.

"I NEED TO TALK TO YOU VERY BAD!" I shouted some more. "'CAUSE I DID A BIG FIB. AND NOW I DON'T KNOW HOW TO GET OUT OF IT!"

Just then Ollie woke up. He started crying very much.

"Great," said Mother very growly.

"Yeah, only sorry, but I'm upset here," I explained.

Ollie screeched louder and louder. His voice sounded like a scratchy sore throat.

Mother put him on her lap. Then she

rubbed the sides of her forehead with her fingers.

That's 'cause she had a mybrain headache, I think.

"You're just going to have to wait until I get the baby settled again," she said, still grumpy.

"Yeah, only I can't wait, 'cause—"

Mother butted in. "Not now, Junie B.! I'll be out to talk to you as soon as I can! Now please go!"

Then she pointed at the door.

Pointing means O-U-T.

"Darn it," I said. "Darn it, darn it, darn it."

'Cause that dumb old baby takes up all of Mother's time.

And he's not even interesting.

He doesn't know how to roll over. Or sit up. Or play Chinese checkers.

He is a dud, I think.

I would like to take him back to the hospital. But Mother said no.

After I left the nursery, I went outside in my front yard.

Then I sat in the grass all by myself. And I played with a stick and another ant.

Only this stupid ant bited me. And so I had to drop a rock on his head.

Finally my daddy's car came into the driveway. And my heart got very happy.

"Daddy's home! Daddy's home! Hurray! Hurray!" I yelled.

Then I ran to him. And he picked me up. And I gave him my most biggest hug.

"I'm very glad to see you!" I said. "'Cause

on Monday I have to dress up like what job I want to be. Except for I accidentally said I'm going to paint and save people and carry lots of keys. Only what kind of dumb bunny job is that?"

My daddy put me down. His eyebrows looked confused at me.

"Can we talk about this at dinner?" he asked.

"No," I said. "We have to talk right now. 'Cause I've already waited all I can. And I'm getting tension in me."

"Well, I'm afraid you're just going to have to wait a little while longer," said Daddy. "Because right now I've got to see if your mother needs help with the baby."

Then he did a kiss on my head. And he walked right into the house!

And guess what?

Sometimes I wish stupid dumb Ollie never even came to live with us.

5/Shining

When I went back inside, Ollie was still very screaming.

That's 'cause Mother couldn't find his pacifier.

Pacifiers are what babies like to suck on. Except I don't know why. 'Cause one time I sucked on Ollie's. And it tasted like my red sneakers.

Just then Mother runned out of Ollie's room.

And her hair was very sticking out.

And her clothes were all wrinkly.

And she was wearing one sock, and that's all.

"WHERE IS IT? WHERE IS THE PACIFIER? IT JUST DIDN'T DISAPPEAR INTO THIN AIR, YOU KNOW!" she hollered very loud.

Then me and Daddy had to help Mother look for the pacifier speedy quick. 'Cause she was losing her grip, I think.

I looked in the couch. That's because sometimes if you push your hand way under the cushions, you can find some good stuff under there.

This time I found three Cheetos and a popcorn.

They were very delicious.

After that, I looked under Daddy's big chair. Only it was too dark to see under there. And so I runned to get the flashlight. 'Cause I learned about flashlights in school, remember?

Flashlights are fun to shine in the dark. I shined it in the dark closet. And also down the dark basement steps.

Then I remembered another dark place. And its name was screaming Ollie's room. 'Cause his shades were pulled down for his nap, that's why.

I runned right there very fast.

"Look," I said to screaming Ollie. "I've got a flashlight."

I shined it on his ceiling.

"See? See that little round circle of shine up there?" I said.

Then I shined it on his jungle wallpaper.

"And see the monkeys, Ollie? And the hippo-pot-of-something?" I asked him.

Only screaming Ollie just kept right on screaming. And he didn't show courtesy to me.

Courtesy is the school word for listening very polite.

That's how come I shined it right in his big fat crying mouth.

Except for just then a problem happened. And it's called Mother sneaked up on me in her quiet sock.

"JUNIE B. JONES! WHAT IN THE WORLD DO YOU THINK YOU'RE DOING?" she hollered.

I did a gulp. Then my heart got very pumpy. Because I was in big trouble, that's why.

"I'm shinin'," I said real soft.

"OUT!" she said. "OUT RIGHT NOW!"

And so that's how come I started to leave. Except for then the flashlight shined on the floor. And I saw something very wonderful down there.

"HEY! LOOK! IT'S THE PACIFIER!" I shouted. "I FOUND THE PACIFIER! IT WAS HIDING UNDER THE ROCKING CHAIR!"

Then I hurried to pick it up. And I gave it to Mother.

Her face got relief on it.

"Thank goodness," she said.

"Yes. Thank goodness," I said back.

Mother wiped the pacifier off. Then she blowed on it very hard.

"Yeah, only you can't blow germs off,

you know," I said. "'Cause stuff that's been on the ground is very dangerous."

And so then Mother gave me the pacifier. And I washed it off with soap and water.

And guess what? Then I put it right in Ollie's mouth. And he stopped crying!

Mother looked proud of me.

"Where did you get so smart?" she asked.

"At school, that's where," I said.

Then all of a sudden my eyes got big and wide. 'Cause a very great idea popped right inside of my head!

"HEY! I THOUGHT OF IT!" I hollered. "I THOUGHT OF WHAT I CAN BE FOR JOB DAY!"

Then I jumped up and down. And I runned down the hall.

Daddy was in his chair reading the paper. I busted through it with my head.

"I THOUGHT OF IT! I THOUGHT OF WHAT KIND OF JOB I CAN BE WHEN I GROW UP!"

Daddy said, "Slow down," to me. That's because he didn't know what the heck I was talking about, of course.

"Yeah, only I can't slow down," I explained. "'Cause I'm very celebrating! And now I don't have tension in me anymore!"

Just then Mother came into the room.

"What's all the excitement about?" she said.

I clapped my hands together. "I have a 'nouncement, that's what it's all about!" I said real happy.

"Well, what is it?" said Mother. "Tell us!"

And so then I stood up straight and tall.

And I told Mother and Daddy the name of the job I'm going to be when I grow up!

"That's a good one, right?" I said very excited. "That's the bestest job you ever heard of, isn't it?"

Except for Mother and Daddy didn't answer me. They just kept on looking and looking at each other.

Then Daddy did a funny smile.

And Mother said the word *ho boy*.

6 / Tingling

I couldn't sleep for the whole weekend. That's because I had tingling excitement in me about Job Day. And my brain wouldn't settle down.

And so on Monday, I zoomed to the bus stop very fast.

"Look, Mr. Woo!" I said to my bus driver. "Look what I'm wearing today!"

Then I opened my jacket and I showed him my job clothes.

"See? It's nice pants. And dangling keys. And a paintbrush," I said. "Except for I can't tell you what I am, 'cause it's my special secret."

Then I plopped down in my seat. And me and Mr. Woo drove to the next corner.

That's where my bestest friend Grace got on.

She was wearing Mickey Mouse ears and a dress with red and white polka dotties on it!

"Grace!" I said very smiling. "You look very beautiful in that dotty thing."

"I know it," she said. "That's because I changed my mind about who I'm going to be when I grow up. Now I'm going to be Minnie instead of Mickey."

Then I stopped smiling. And my stomach felt very sickish inside again.

'Cause that meant Minnie Mouse was a fake too.

"Disneyland is a fib," I said.

After that, the bus stopped again. And William got on.

He was wearing a Superman outfit. Except he had a W on the front of him. And not the letter S.

"The W stands for William," he said to Mr. Woo.

"Does that mean you can fly?" asked Mr. Woo.

Then William grinned very big. And he held out his arms. And he jumped way high in the air.

Except for he didn't fly.

And so he just sat down.

After that, other kids got on the bus, too.

And Roger had on keys just like me. And also plastic handcuffs.

And Charlotte was wearing a red paint apron with some watercolors in the pocket.

And that mean Jim was wearing a white bathrobe.

"Hey! I've got a bathrobe just like that, Jim!" I said very friendly.

"It's not a bathrobe, dummy," he said. "I'm a kung fu karate guy."

"Jim is a kung fu karate guy," I said to Grace. "Except for he just got out of the bathtub."

Then me and her laughed and laughed. 'Cause that was a funny joke, of course.

And Job Day was going to be the funnest day in the whole wide world!

7/Jobs and Jobs

When I got off the bus, I zoomed to Room Nine. That's because I wanted Job Day to start very quick.

Only first we had to take attendance.

And then we had to say *I pledge allegiance to the flag of the United States of America, and to the republic for which it stands.*

Except I don't know what that dumb story is even talking about.

Then finally Mrs. clapped her loud hands together.

And guess what? Job Day started, that's what!

"Boys and girls, you all look wonderful in your outfits!" Mrs. said. "I can't wait to learn what all of you want to be when you grow up! Who would like to go first?"

"I WOULD! I WOULD!" I yelled out.

Only then my bestest friend Lucille raised her hand very polite. And she got to go first.

Lucille looked the most beautifulest I've ever seen her.

She was wearing a new dress that her nanna bought for her. It was the color of pink velvet.

Also she had on shiny pink shoes. And socks with bows and lace on them.

Lucille's nanna is loaded, I think.

Lucille went to the front of the room. She reached into a little bag and pulled out a sparkling crown with jewels on it!

Then all of Room Nine said, "Ooooooh."

Except for not the boys.

"When I grow up, I'm going to marry a prince," she said. "And I'll be a princess. And my name will be Princess Lucille."

Then she put the sparkling crown on her head. And she looked like a fairy tale guy.

Mrs. smiled. "That's a lovely thought, Lucille," she said.

"I know," said Lucille. "My nanna says if you marry a prince, you're set for life."

After that, Lucille said her dress costed eighty-five. And her shoes costed forty-five. And her lacy socks costed six fifty plus tax.

Then Mrs. told Lucille to sit down.

Ricardo went next.

He was wearing a round yellow hat. It was the kind of hat you can bang on.

"This is called a hard hat," he said. "You have to wear it when you're building tall buildings. Or else somebody might drop a hammer from way up high. And it could hit you on the head and kill you."

Mrs. smiled. "So you're interested in construction, right, Ricardo?" she asked.

But Ricardo just kept on talking about other stuff that could fall on your head and kill you. Like a paint can. And an electric drill. And a lunchbox.

Then Mrs. said, "Sit down," to him, too.

That's when William raised his hand. Only he was being very bashful. And he wouldn't go to the front of the room.

"You don't have to be nervous, William," said Mrs. "Just tell us what you want to be when you grow up."

William covered his face with his hands.

"Super William," he said very quiet.

Then he got out of his seat. And he jumped way high in the air. Only his cape got tangled up in his chair. And he crashed into the table.

After that, Super William got very sniffling. And Mrs. said we would get back to him later.

Then lots of other kids talked about their jobs.

Like a boy named Clifton is going to be a rich and famous astronaut.

And a girl named Lily is going to be a rich and famous movie star. And also she wants to direct.

And a boy named Ham is going to be a rich and famous boss of a big company. And he taught us how to say the word *you're fired*.

And here's the bestest one of all! 'Cause a boy named Jamal Hall is going to be the rich and famous president of the whole United States!

"Cool!" said Ricardo.

Then the other boys said, "Cool," too.

I did a secret smile. Yeah, only not as cool as my job, I thought to just myself.

Then I raised my hand very polite. And Mrs. called my name.

"OH, BOY!" I shouted. "OH, BOY! OH, BOY! 'CAUSE MINE IS EVEN BETTER THAN PRESIDENT OF THE UNITED STATES!"

I zoomed speedy quick to the front of the room.

Then my excitement wouldn't stay inside of me anymore.

"A JANITOR! I'M GOING TO BE A JANITOR!" I hollered out.

After that, I jingled my jangly keys! And I waved my paintbrush in the air! And I clapped and clapped!

Only too bad for me.

'Cause nobody clapped back.

And here's something even worser.

Room Nine started laughing very much. And it was the mean kind.

"SHE WANTS TO BE A JANITOR!" they yelled.

Then they pointed at my brown pants.

And they called me the name of stupid.

And I didn't know what to do. 'Cause I felt very crumbling inside.

And so I just kept on standing there and standing there.

And my eyes got a little bit of wet in them. And my nose started running very much.

That's how come I covered my face up.

"They're not having courtesy for me," I said real soft.

Only just then Mrs. clapped her angry hands together. And she scolded Room Nine a real lot.

"Junie B. is right," she said. "Being a janitor is a very important job. You have to be hardworking and reliable and very, very trustworthy."

I peeked through my fingers at her.

"Yeah, and don't forget the part where you have to save people from danger," I said.

Then that Jim I hate laughed right out loud. "Janitors don't save people from danger, you goonie bird!" he said.

I stamped my foot at him. "Yes, they do! They do too! Because one time I was eating a dangerous Life Saver. And Janitor made me spit it out! And also he brought his flashlight to Room Nine. And he saved William from the dangerous dental floss!"

Then I held up my jingling keys.

"And see these things? Keys are what Janitor unlocks the bathroom door with. Or else we couldn't even go to the toilet!"

Then I showed him my paintbrush.

"And Janitor paints litter cans, too," I said. "And painting is the funnest thing I love!"

That Jim did a mean smile. "Yeah, well, too bad for you, but you're a girl. And janitors have to be boys. So there."

I runned to his table. "No, they do not,

you stupid head Jim!" I said. "Girls can be anything boys can be! Right, Mrs.? Right? Right? 'Cause I saw that on *Sesame Street*. And also on *Oprah*."

Mrs. did a smile.

Then my bestest friend Grace started to clap.

And guess what? All of the other girls in Room Nine clapped too.

8/Gus Vallony

Today Janitor came to Room Nine for Show and Tell!

And it was the funnest day I ever saw!

That's 'cause he brought his very big tool-box with him.

And we played a game called Name the Tools.

And guess what?

I knew the saw.

And the hammer.

And the metric socket set with adjustable ratchet.

Then Janitor showed us how to use his stuff.

And Charlotte got to shine his giant flashlight.

And my bestest friend Grace got to push his big broom.

And lucky duck Lucille got to clean the chalkboard with his squishy sponge.

Except for then a little bit of trouble happened. 'Cause I wanted the mop. Only that stupid head Jim wouldn't let go of it. And so I had to pinch his arm.

After that, the mop got removed from us.

Removed is the school word for snatched right out of our hands.

After that, Janitor sat in a chair. And Room Nine sat all around him.

Then he told us all about himself and his job.

And guess what?

He's been Janitor for fourteen years.

And he was borned in a different country from ours.

And his name is Gus Vallony!

"Hey! I love that name of Gus Vallony!" I hollered out. "'Cause Vallony is my favorite kind of sandwich!"

Then I smiled very proud.

"And guess what else?" I said to Room Nine. "Me and Janitor are bestest friends. And sometimes he calls me the nickname of sis!"

Then Janitor winked at me.

And so I winked back. Except for both my eyes kept on shutting. And so I had to hold one of them open with my fingers.

"I really like that Gus Vallony," I whispered to my bestest friend Lucille.

Only then that dumb girl named Lily heard what I said.

And she started singing, *"Junie B.'s got a boyyy friennnd. Junie B.'s got a boyyy friennnd."*

And so that's how come I felt very embarrassed.

"Me and my big fat mouth!" I said.

Then Mrs. laughed.

And Janitor laughed.

And everybody else laughed too.

After that, Janitor had to go back to work. And so Mrs. shook his hand.

Then Room Nine clapped and clapped for him.

And Janitor smiled.

And his jingly keys jangled all the way out the door.

kindergarten

Kindergarten is what comes before first grade. Except for I don't know why it's named that dumb word of kindergarten. 'Cause it should be named zero grade, I think.

work

Work is when you use your brain and a pencil. Only sometimes I accidentally use the eraser too hard. And a hole comes in my paper.

the grocery store

Saturday is the day me and my mother go to the grocery store. It is very fun at that place. Except for no hollering I WANT ICE CREAM! And no calling Mother the name of big meanie.

Mrs.

I wish Mrs. lived next door to me. Then me and her would be neighbors. And bestest friends. And also I could spy on her.

spying

I am a very good spier. That's because I have sneaky feet. And my nose doesn't whistle when I breathe.

the water fountain

No putting your mouth on the water spout. Or else germs will get inside you. And you will die.

secrets

Nobody can see secrets inside your head. Not even if they look in your ears.

About the Author

Barbara Park is no stranger to occupational indecision. When she was in kindergarten, she wanted to be a dancer. Or an ice skater. Or a wallpaper hanger.

"No matter how mediocre I was at something, my mother always thought I was great," says Barbara Park. "When I learned to skate backwards, she was ready to sign me up for the Ice Capades."

Barbara Park finally decided to become a writer, and thousands of readers are glad she did. She has received many awards for her hilarious children's books, including seven children's choice awards and four *Parents' Choice* awards. She lives in Arizona with her husband, Richard, and their two sons, Steven and David.